MY BROWN BEAR BARNEY AT THE PARTY

By Dorothy Butler
Pictures by Elizabeth Fuller

GREENWILLOW BOOKS
An Imprint of HarperCollinsPublishers

For my granddaughter Phoebe —D.B.

For Georgia —E.F.

Pen and ink and watercolors were used for the full-color art.
The text type is Goudy Old Style BT.

My Brown Bear Barney at the Party
Text copyright © 2001 by Dorothy Butler
Illustrations copyright © 2001 by Elizabeth Fuller
All rights reserved.
Printed in Hong Kong by South China Printing Company (1988) Ltd.
www.harperchildrens.com

Library of Congress Cataloging-in-Publication Data

Butler, Dorothy, (date)
My brown bear Barney at the party / by Dorothy Butler.
p. cm.
"Greenwillow Books."
Summary: Barney the brown bear accompanies his owner to Harold Hinkel's birthday
party, where he suffers several indignities at the hands of Harold's little sister Poppy.
ISBN 0-688-17548-1 (trade).   ISBN 0-688-17549-X (lib. bdg.)
[1. Teddy bears—Fiction. 2. Parties—Fiction. 3. Birthdays—Fiction.]
I. Title.   PZ7.B976 Myg   2001   [E]—dc21   00-021057

1 2 3 4 5 6 7 8 9 10   First Printing

My friend Fred and I are excited.
We have been invited to Harold Hinkel's birthday party!
Harold says we must wear party clothes and have good manners.
My brown bear Barney hasn't been invited, but he's going anyway.

We spend a long time choosing Harold Hinkel's presents.
I choose a red flashlight for him, and my friend Fred
chooses a box of paints.

My father drives us to the party.
I am wearing my new green dress with pockets like mermaids,
and Fred is wearing his best T-shirt with a rocket on the back.
My father is wearing his old gardening T-shirt with a hole in the front.

Harold Hinkel and his mother meet us at their front door,
and we give Harold his presents.
Then we go upstairs to see his other presents.

Fred and I are amazed. Harold Hinkel's bed is covered with presents!
He likes ours, though, especially the flashlight. Harold's little sister
Poppy thinks my brown bear Barney is *her* present!
She screams and screams, and I have to let her hold him.
Barney doesn't mind.

We all go down to play in the garden.
Harold Hinkel's garden has a hammock in it.
Fred and I pretend the hammock is a pirate ship, and we are the pirates.
I am the captain, and Fred is the mate. Harold can be the cook.

Then we swing and swing. Our ship is in a big storm at sea.
"Heave-ho, me hearties!" shouts Fred.
Harold is scared, but I'm not.
Barney is missing all the fun, though.

Harold Hinkel's mother comes running out.
"Stop! Stop!" she shouts.
Too late.
Our ship capsizes, and we are hurled into the sea!

My friend Fred lands on the concrete path
and skins one of his knees and scrapes both his elbows.
I land in the vegetable garden on top of the lettuces.
Harold lands on the grass, but he bawls very loudly.

Mrs. Hinkel picks Harold up from the lawn,
and Fred and I pick ourselves up.
Mrs. Hinkel brushes some of the dirt off me
and puts Band-Aids on Fred.
Then she tells Mr. Hinkel to take the hammock down this minute.
Then she says, "Where's Poppy?"

Poppy is lost—and so is my brown bear Barney!
We all hunt for them.
We hunt in the garden, and we hunt in the house.
No Poppy! No Barney!
Then we all hear Harold Hinkel scream.
Everyone rushes up to his bedroom.

Oh, no! There is Poppy, and there is Barney, and there is
Fred's present with all the tubes of paint squeezed out.
Poppy has painted my brown bear Barney and herself yellow
and red and blue and all the other colors of the rainbow!

Mr. Hinkel takes Poppy away to clean her up,
and Mrs. Hinkel gives Barney a bath in the sink.
She washes his ribbon and then dries him with her hair dryer.
Barney looks all fluffy, and not nearly as brown as usual.

Now it is time to eat.
In the Hinkels' dining room there is an aquarium.
We all watch the little colored fish darting in and out
among the rocks and plants.
Poppy holds my brown bear Barney up so that he can see.
(Will I ever get him back?)

At last we are eating the scrumptious food.
We all have party hats and whistles and balloons.
Harold Hinkel blows out his birthday candles,
and we all sing, "Happy birthday, dear Harold."
Poppy stands on her chair and holds Barney
up high again so that he can see.

Oh, no!
Poppy has thrown my brown bear Barney in with the fish!
He sinks to the bottom, and the water spills over the top.
Barney gazes sadly out through the glass.

I run quickly to rescue him. I have to stand on a chair, but I manage
to haul him out by one ear. Lots of the little colored fish come, too,
and more water and quite a few plants.
Everyone else rushes to rescue the little fish and put them back.
They all think this is the best part of the party, but Barney and I don't!

Harold Hinkel's mother takes Barney away to wash and dry him *again*,
and we all play a game in the living room.
Fred and I want to play leapfrog, but Mr. Hinkel says, "*No.*"
We must play a quiet game.
So we play "Simon Says," but it does not turn out to be *very* quiet.

Harold Hinkel's mother brings Barney back, looking even cleaner
and fluffier than before. She sits him on top of a very high
bookcase where none of us can reach him.
Poor old Barney!
Poppy screams and *screams*, and her father takes her away somewhere.
We can still hear her, though.

When it is Fred's turn to be Simon, he says,
"Simon says, 'Stand on your head!'"
Harold Hinkel isn't very good at standing on his head,
and he knocks over a vase of flowers.
The glass doesn't break, though.

My father comes to collect us. He is now wearing
a nice clean shirt. He looks surprised when he sees us.
"How come you two look so battered, and Barney looks so clean?" he asks.
We don't tell him. We just laugh and laugh.
My father would like to thank Mrs. Hinkel,
but Mr. Hinkel says she is lying down.

Soon we are on our way home.
"That was the best party I ever went to," says my friend Fred.
"Me, too," I say.
My brown bear Barney just sits there smiling.